The Caring Me I Want To Be!

by Mary DiPalermo

Illustrated by Emma Randall

SCHOLASTIC INC.

To Laura Bryn and Laura D.,
your kindness and caring helped this book be!
—M. D.

To Mum and Dad, who always taught me to be kind.
—x, E. R.

Text copyright © 2018 by Mary DiPalermo.
Illustrations copyright © by Scholastic Inc.

ISBN 978-1-338-25425-9

18   21 22

Printed in the U.S.A.   40
First printing 2018

Book design by Jennifer Rinaldi

The caring me I want to be is filled with possibilities!

I'm up. I'm bright. I say *Hello!* to all the people that I know.

I share a smile. I listen well.

I'm kind, as everyone can tell.

I hug my pup.

I help my sis.

Being me—it feels like this!

Kind acts have amazing powers.

I've seen them work—
they last for hours!

When our crossing guard had the flu,
a bunch of daisies helped him feel new.

Kind words from my favorite teacher . . .

... make me feel proud—I'm a special creature!

When friends are kind,
I'm cheerful, too.

We all feel good.
We stick like glue.

Kindness has a way of spreading.

It starts with me. It's never-ending!

And yet . . .

There are days I do not show
the me that seems to spread that glow.

I scrunch my brow. I raise my voice.

I act as if I have no choice.

Then I remember . . . I *do* have a choice.

Being kind, it feels so good.
It makes me happy (and it should!).

Nothing cures my bad mood faster—or saves
a playdate from disaster—than being fair and gentle, too.
I do the best that I can do.

If someone has a face that's sad,
I try to make her sad face glad!

What makes a friendship truly real
is thinking of how others feel.

All these things, they help me see
the caring me I want to be!

About this Book:

The Caring Me I Want To Be was developed to introduce young children to the incredible power of kindness. Being kind is a choice that makes both the giver and the receiver feel great. In addition, kind acts have a way of spreading—when you're kind to someone, they're likely to be kind to somebody else!

Parents can use this story at home to help guide social skills. Teachers can use this book at school to start group discussions about caring, kindness, and building community.

Helpful Tips:

⭐ Remind kids how good it feels when someone is kind to them. Ask them to give examples of the last time someone was kind and how that felt. Did it improve their mood? Their day? Ask them to think of the kind things they've done to help others.

⭐ Talk about the opposite, too. Discuss how it feels when people don't choose kindness.

⭐ Create a kindness challenge. Keep a visible list of the kind acts you do. Try to add to that list every day. When you get to a certain number (5? 10? 25?) celebrate! Throw a dance party, read an extra book at story time, share some jelly beans . . . whatever it is that makes you feel good.

⭐ Encourage your child to notice the kind acts they see at home, at school, at the store, around town, everywhere! Let kids know that being kind—even talking about kindness and keeping kind thoughts—is a sure way to share happiness.

Remember, kindness is contagious!